For Catherine

PUFFIN BOOKS

Published by the Penguin Group
Penguin Books Ltd, 27 Wrights Lane, London W8 5TZ, England
Penguin Books USA Inc., 375 Hudson Street, New York, New York 10014, USA
Penguin Books Australia Ltd, Ringwood, Victoria, Australia
Penguin Books Canada Ltd, 10 Alcorn Avenue, Toronto, Ontario, Canada M4V 3B2
Penguin Books (NZ) Ltd, Private Bag 102902, NSMC, Auckland, New Zealand

On the World Wide Web at: www.penguin.com

Penguin Books Ltd, Registered Offices: Harmondsworth, Middlesex, England

First published by Viking 1999
Published in Puffin Books 2000
1 3 5 7 9 10 8 6 4 2

Copyright © John Wallace, 1999
All rights reserved

The moral right of the author/illustrator has been asserted

Set in Comic Sans

Printed in Hong Kong by Wing King Tong Co. Ltd.

British Library Cataloguing in Publication Data
A CIP catalogue record for this book is available from the British Library

ISBN 0-140-56555-8

249866

it to be returned on before

TINY Rabbit

Goes to a Birthday Party

John Wallace

PUFFIN BOOKS

A special letter had arrived in the post for Tiny Rabbit. He opened it.
"It's an invitation to Blue Mouse's birthday party!" said Tiny Rabbit.
"Brilliant!"

Tiny Rabbit was *so* excited – he'd
never been to a party before.
He phoned Pig to find out what
happened at parties. Tiny Rabbit
had a lot to do to get ready!

First, Tiny Rabbit needed to choose something to wear. He tried on his favourite outfits...

Fire bunny...

Doctor...

Bat bunny . . .

"I know!" said Tiny Rabbit. "I'll just go as myself."

Next, Tiny Rabbit had to find the perfect present. What would Blue Mouse *really* like?

A carrot?

A picture?

Some lettuce?

"I know!" said
Tiny Rabbit.

"I'll give him . . .

...this big cardboard box!"

Tiny Rabbit started to wrap up the box.

It was a bit
tricky . . .

and he got a
bit sticky . . .

but he managed
in the end.

On the way to Blue Mouse's party,
Tiny Rabbit began thinking.

"What if I don't know anyone?
What if I don't like the food?
What if I want to go home?"

By the time he got to the party,
Tiny Rabbit was feeling a bit scared.
He wasn't sure he'd enjoy himself.
"I think I'll just stay
here and watch,"
thought Tiny Rabbit.

But then Blue Mouse saw Tiny Rabbit and came over.
"Happy birthday," whispered Tiny Rabbit, feeling very shy. "Here's your present."

"Wow! Thank you," said Blue Mouse,
and started to unwrap the big,
mysterious present.
"It's a box! I love it!" cried Blue
Mouse.

Everyone started playing with the box.

They climbed
into it . . .

scrambled
through it . . .

and hid
inside it.

Tiny Rabbit thought it looked like fun,
but didn't think he wanted to join in.

When the real games started,
Stripey Cat held out his paw
and said, "Come on, Tiny Rabbit.
Come and play!"

Soon Tiny Rabbit stopped feeling
shy and joined in.

Then it was time for tea. Tiny Rabbit
had a bit of everything, and even
tried some things he'd never
had before.

Stripey Cat ate so much
that he fell off his chair.

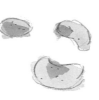

Next, Blue Mouse had to make a wish while he blew out all the candles on his birthday cake. All his friends counted, "One ... two ... three ..." Whoosh!

Blue Mouse didn't blow quite hard enough, so Tiny Rabbit joined in to help. Tiny Rabbit really had to huff and puff, but he managed in the end.

All too soon it was the end of the party. Tiny Rabbit had forgotten how he'd felt when he first arrived, and went home feeling very full and very happy.

When he got home, Tiny Rabbit had lots to do. It would be *his* birthday in four weeks and two days, and he had a birthday party to plan!